A GOLDEN BOOK • NEW YORK

Library of Congress Control Number: 2007926583
ISBN: 978-0-375-84580-2
www.goldenbooks.com
www.randomhouse.com/kids
PRINTED IN SINGAPORE
10 9 8 7 6 5 4 3
First Random House Edition 2008

GOOD NIGHT, LITTLE BEAR

It is time for Little Bear to go to bed.
Mother Bear closes the storybook.
She gives Little Bear a good-night kiss.

Then over to
his big furry father
runs the little bear.

Wheee!

Father Bear swings his little one high up
to his shoulders for a ride to bed.

"Duck your head," calls Mother Bear, just in time.
And into the snug little bedroom they go.

Squeak!
The tiny bed sighs as Father Bear sits down.
"Now, into bed with you," he says.
He waits for Little Bear to climb down.
But Little Bear doesn't move.
He sits up on his father's shoulders and grins.
Father Bear waits. He yawns a rumbly yawn.
Is Father Bear falling asleep?
No. Suddenly he opens his eyes again.

"Why, I must have been dreaming,"
says Father Bear, pretending to wake up.
But what's this?
There is no furry head on the pillow.
Where can Little Bear be?
Father Bear looks under the pillow.
Nobody there.
He doesn't seem to feel
something tickling his ear.

Aha.
There's a lump down under the blanket.
Father Bear pats the lump.
But it doesn't squeak or wiggle.
Can it be Little Bear?

Why, it's the toy teddy and the blue bunny waiting for Little Bear to come to bed!

"Mother, that naughty bear is hiding,"
says Father Bear to Mother Bear, with a wink.
"Maybe he's hiding under the kitchen stove,"
says Mother Bear, who loves a joke.

Bang! Bang!
Father Bear rattles the pots and pans
on top of the stove.
"Little Bear, I'm coming to get you!" he roars.

Father Bear reaches under the stove.
He feels something soft and furry.
Is it Little Bear?

No.
It's only Father Bear's old winter mitten.

'Way up high Little Bear claps his paw
to his mouth. But not in time.
"I heard that Little Bear laugh," says Father.
"Now where can he be hiding?"

"Is he standing outside the front door?
I'll turn the knob softly—
and fling the door wide!"
No. There are no bears out there.
Just a family of fat little rabbits
nibbling lettuce in the garden.
"Shoo!" snorts Father Bear.

"Something is hiding in the woodbox,"
whispers Mother Bear.
"Creep over there on tip toe,
and you may catch a little bear."
Eeek!
There's just a wee mouse hiding there.

There's nobody up high, on the china shelf.
"Ouch!"
Little Bear bumps his head.
"Who said Ouch?" asks Father Bear.
"Mother, did you say Ouch?"
"Not I," smiles Mother Bear.
Oh she is a tease.

"Now where is that naughty bear hiding?
He wouldn't run away.
Not a little bear who is always hungry
for chocolate cake."
And that big Daddy Bear cuts himself a huge piece
of chocolate cake right under the little bear's nose.

Little Bear suddenly feels hungry.
But just then Father Bear stops smack
in front of the mirror.
"Why, there he is," roars the big bear.
"But you couldn't find me," squeaks Little Bear,
reaching for chocolate cake.

Wheee!
Off Daddy's shoulders and down to the sofa.
Bounce. Bounce. Bounce.
"Wasn't that a good hiding place, Mommy?
No one could find me up there."

"But I've found you now," says Father Bear.
Little Bear wiggles and giggles under his Daddy's
strong arm . . . all the way into bed.

"Did I really fool you, Daddy?"
asks Little Bear.
Father Bear just laughs and winks.
Do you think Father Bear knew all the time?

CHIPMUNK'S

A

B

C

A is for **apple tree**.

B is for **burrow**. Guess who lives in the **burrow** under the apple tree?

C is for **Chipmunk**. It is **Chipmunk** who lives in the burrow under the apple tree.

D is for **Donkey**. Chipmunk and **Donkey** have been out picking **daffodils**.

E is for **ears**. Chipmunk's mother
washes his **ears**.

F is for **friends**. Chipmunk has several
good **friends**. **Froggie** is a **friend**.

G is for Goat.

Goat plays a **game** with Chipmunk.

H is for **hide-and-seek**. Chipmunk and his friends **hide** in **holes** and **hedges**.

I is for **ice cream**.

Donkey is serving **ice cream**.

J is for **jump**. Froggie **jumps** for **joy**. He loves ice cream.

K is for **kitchen**. Chipmunk puts the **kettle** on. Mouse is slicing cheese with a **knife**.

L is for **lake**. Chipmunk and Bunny go sailing on the **lake**. Both wear **life** jackets.

M is for **mumps**. **Mouse** has **mumps**.
He listens to **music** and has **meals** in bed.

N is for **net**.
Chipmunk catches butterflies in his **net**.
Then he lets them go.

O is for **oboe**. Froggie plays the **oboe**.
Donkey drinks from an **orange** cup.

P is for **party**.

Chipmunk loves **parties**. Mouse is over
the mumps. He has brought Chipmunk a
present, a bunch of **pansies**.

Q is for **quilt**.
Chipmunk's mother is making a **quilt**.

R is for **river**, where Chipmunk and Donkey have a swimming **race**.

S is for **swing**.

Chipmunk likes to **swing** almost as much as he likes to **swim**.

T is for **telephone**.

Someone wants to **talk** to Chipmunk.

U is for **umbrella** to keep out the sun.

V is for **vacation**. Chipmunk is at the seashore, staying in a **villa** with a nice **view** of the sea.

W is for **wagon**. Goat pulls the **wagon**, and Chipmunk rides. The **weather** is nice, and they have a **watermelon** to eat.

X is a letter. Chipmunk and Bunny play
tic-tac-toe with an **X** and an O.

Y is for **yellow**. **Yellow** flowers grow in Chipmunk's **yard**.

Z is for **zipper**. Chipmunk **zips** his jacket.
He is going outside to play with his friends.

THE DADDY BUNNY tossed his baby in the air.

"What will our baby be when he grows up?" asked the daddy bunny.

"He will be a policeman with gold buttons on his suit," said the mother bunny. "He will help little lost children find their mothers and daddies."

"Maybe he will be a circus clown," said the daddy bunny. "He will wear a funny suit and do funny tricks to make the children laugh."

"Why can't our baby be a cowboy?" asked the bunny brother. "If he grows up to be a cowboy he can ride horses at the rodeo."

But the baby bunny did not want to be a policeman or
a circus clown or a cowboy when he grew up.

He sat in his basket and smiled at his bunny family. He
knew what he would be.

"I think our baby bunny should be an airplane pilot,"
said the little bunny sister. "He could fly into the sky.
And when he felt like having fun he could jump out in
his parachute."

"Maybe he will be a fireman," said his Great Aunt Bunny. "Then he could drive a big ladder truck to all the fires. He would be a brave fireman."

Great Uncle Bunny wanted the baby to be an engineer on a big train.

"He would ring the bell when he was ready to start the train. And blow his horn, Toot! Toot! in the tunnels," said Great Uncle Bunny.

But the baby bunny did not want to be an airplane pilot or a fireman or an engineer on a big train when he grew up. He nibbled on his carrot and looked wise. He knew what he wanted to be.

Old Grandaddy Bunny said:
"Just look at that baby. Why, any bunny can see he is going to be a lion tamer!"

But Grandma Bunny said:
"I think he will be a nice little mailman who will bring
a letter to every house and make the neighbors happy."

A hungry little bunny cousin wished that the baby would have a candy store.

"He could make lollypops with funny faces and give them to all the good children," wished the hungry little bunny cousin.

But the baby bunny did not want to be a
lion tamer or a mailman or have a candy store.
He shook his rattle and smiled.
He would be what he wanted to be.

The little girl cousin said:
  "It would be nice if our baby was a doctor. Then he
could put big bandages on little bumps."

"Oh dear no," said Aunt Bunny. "I am sure he will be a
lifeguard at the beach. He will save people who can't swim."

"Not at all, my dear," said Uncle Bunny. "This little baby may grow up to be a farmer with a fine red tractor."

But the baby bunny did not want to be a doctor or a
lifeguard or a farmer with a fine red tractor when he grew up.
He bounced on his daddy's knee and laughed.
Can you guess what he will be?

The baby bunny will be a daddy rabbit!
That is what he will be—with lots of little bunny
children to feed when they are hungry.

He will be a nice daddy who will chase the children
when they want to be chased.

And give them presents on their birthdays.

He will read them a story when they are sleepy.

And tuck them into bed at night.
And that is what the baby bunny will grow up to be.
A daddy rabbit.